E
Pr

Primavera, Elise
Basil and Maggie

$7.49

DATE DUE

OC 23 8	JY 22 7	
MR 9 '90	OC 11 7	
AG 14 '91		
APR 16 '9		
JUN 22 '9		
SEP 15 '9		
AP 18 '00		
AG 02 '0		
SE 10 0		
OC 08 '02		
AG 11 '03		
NO 06 '03		

Basil & Maggie

Elise Primavera

J.B. Lippincott / New York

For Betsy Isele and Slim

Maggie took riding lessons three times a week. "Up down, up down, keep your chin up, put your heels down," the riding instructor would call out. Everyone was getting ready for the big horse show on Saturday!

On the way to her lesson, Maggie and her dog, Pippin, stopped at her mailbox. Inside was a letter from her Aunt Isabel, who lived in England.

The letter said:

Dear Maggie

Since I heard how keen you are on riding, I have decided to send you my best pony—his name is Basil. The climate here on the moors is quite rainy, and the ground is ever so muddy, but Basil can bounce through the worst of it!

Take good care of him, he's a very special pony.

All my love,
Your Aunt Isabel

Basil was coming to America on a boat. Maggie could hardly wait to meet him.

"We'll win everything on Saturday," she thought. "The other kids won't believe their eyes when they see me ride in on my fancy new English pony!"

Suddenly Maggie saw something trot down the gangplank.

"This can't be Basil," she said. "He's too hairy, too fat, and just look at those big feet!" Basil walked up to Maggie and smiled shyly.

"He looks like two men in a horse costume!" she cried. And he did.

Maggie gave Basil a bath as soon as she got him home and settled in his new barn. It took gallons of water. She curried him and brushed him, and cut a foot of hair off his tail. Then she stood back to admire her new pony.

"That's much better," she said. "Tomorrow we start training for the show."

The minute Maggie got on Basil, he began his bounciest, proudest trot.

"St-stop st-sto-op-op-op!" Maggie screamed. "No, no, no, Basil, you can't trot like that in a show. You have to prick your ears, trot long and close to the ground, and then flick your toes."

Hours later, Maggie finally gave up on the trot.

"All right," she said, "so your trot is not so great. But you ought to be a really good show jumper, Basil, because you're so bouncy!" Hours later, Maggie gave up on the jumping.

It was the night before the horse show. Maggie had spent the day cleaning her saddle and bridle, braiding Basil's mane and worrying.

"I still don't think he knows what I'm talking about, Pippin. The show is tomorrow, and that stupid pony doesn't do anything right!"

The next morning, Maggie led Basil into the trailer.
He looked as gloomy as the dark clouds that hung in
the sky.

"Don't worry, Basil," Maggie said, trying to cheer him up. "No matter how this turns out, I'll still love you." She put up the tailgate, shut the side door, and looked into the window at him.

"But *please*, just try not to bounce."

When Maggie and Basil walked into the ring, everyone laughed and pointed.

"Look at his ears!" said one. "His ears? Look at those feet!" said another.

"Don't listen to them," said Maggie. "Just remember all the things I told you to do."

"Trot please! All trot!" the judges said, as the first class began. Basil took a deep breath and started. He got his head down just fine, but his legs kept popping up and then his ears started to flop around. He completely forgot to flick his toes.

When the ribbons were handed out, Maggie and
Basil were the only ones who didn't get a prize.

"That's all right, Basil," Maggie said, trying to look at the bright side. "We've still got one more class, and it's only raining a little. Things can't get worse."

It began to pour.

"Number 7," called the gatekeeper.

"That's us, Basil!" Maggie cried.

They bounced through the glop past all the other horses who were slipping and sliding in the gooey mud. Maggie and Basil sprang onto the outside course.

A hush fell over the crowd as they watched Basil trot through the sticky mud toward the first fence.

Everyone cheered and clapped as Basil cleared the
first jump and then all the others after.

"Ahem," said the judges, stepping forward.

"In our most professional and respected opinions as
official judges, we have decided that Basil deserves
first prize!"

That night, Maggie filled the silver bowl with hot
bran mash and carrots and carried it to Basil's stall.
"This is for my very special pony," Maggie said.

Library of Congress Cataloging in Publication Data
Primavera, Elise.
    Basil and Maggie.

Summary: Maggie wants a show horse but gets Basil
instead, and discovers that this lumpy pony is
something special.
1. Ponies—Juvenile fiction.   [1. Ponies—Fiction]
I. Title.
PZ10.3.P9254Bas 1983   [E]   82-48455
ISBN 0-397-32027-2
ISBN 0-397-32028-0 (lib. bdg.)

1 2 3 4 5 6 7 8 9 10
First Edition